YOUNG WIZARDS

Michael Lawrence

Illustrated by Chris Mould

For Erin

First published in 2008 in Great Britain by
Barrington Stoke Ltd
18 Walker Street, Edinburgh, EH3 7LP

www.barringtonstoke.co.uk

This edition first published 2014

Text © 2008 Michael Lawrence
Illustrations © Chris Mould

The moral right of Michael Lawrence and Chris Mould to
be identified as the author and illustrator of this work has
been asserted in accordance with the Copyright, Designs
and Patents Act, 1988

A CIP catalogue record for this book is available
from the British Library upon request

ISBN: 978-1-78112-356-0

Printed in China by Leo

Contents

Chapter 1
Strange Things

Let me start by telling you that there was no magic on the Wizard Lea Estate. Wizard Lea was as un-magical as any housing estate can be. Oh, it was nice enough. The houses were modern, the gardens were neat, and most of the cars that stood in the driveways or at the kerbs weren't very old. But of real magic there wasn't a drop.

And this was the very thing that had drawn Mr and Mrs Pertinax to it. Well, that and its name, of course.

"The Wizard Lea Estate," they said when they heard of it. "Oh, we must move there."

So, almost a year ago, that's what they did.

Mr and Mrs Pertinax had three children – a girl and two boys. Ellie, the girl, was the eldest. The boys were twins, called Brin and Arlo. This story begins on the Friday morning that Brin and Arlo became eleven years and six months of age.

Now, becoming eleven years and six months of age is nothing special. For one thing, as it's slap-bang between birthdays eleven and twelve, you don't get presents and cards. The twins might not have minded this if it hadn't been the day before Ellie's 13th birthday. The day she would be getting all the things that they would not.

"Why the long faces?" their mother asked when they went down to breakfast that morning.

"Want a birthday tomorrow," Brin said glumly.

"Well, you can't have a birthday tomorrow," Mrs Pertinax replied. "Anyway, I think eleven and a half is quite old enough for two growing boys to be getting on with."

As she said this, she looked at her husband, who was eating his toast and reading the morning paper. He looked worried.

Mr Pertinax said, "Apart from being jealous of your sister's birthday tomorrow, do you two feel ... all right?"

"No," said Arlo. "We're fed up."

"Not yet, you're not," said Mum. "Sit down and eat your breakfast."

They sat down. While they ate,
Ellie smirked at them across the table.
"Tomorrow," the smirk seemed to say, "I'll
have a birthday and you won't."

It was because of that smirk that, after
breakfast, Brin and Arlo made up their minds
to give their sister a very un-special present
tomorrow.

They found it in the cupboard under
the stairs, at the back of a shelf covered in
cobwebs. It was the most un-special present
you could think of. Their late grandmother's
dustpan and brush. It was so old and worn
that it hadn't been used for years.

"Tee-hee," they said, as they sneaked the
dustpan and brush upstairs. In their room,
they wrapped it in some left-over Christmas
paper and put it under one of their beds.

Finding and wrapping the un-special
present cheered the twins up so much that

when their friends called for them, they were quite happy to go to school, for a change.

Mr and Mrs Pertinax, still very worried, watched them go.

It was at school that morning that strange things started to happen.

The first strange thing happened in Maths. Mr Choi had set the class a test. He had filled the board with sums that he wanted everyone to try and work out before the end of the lesson.

"Is there a reward for anyone who gets them all right, sir?" Harry Pooter asked.

"Yes," said Mr Choi. "A shocked grin from me. Go on – impress me!"

The class had been working on the sums for about five minutes when the Deputy Head looked in. There was a phone call in the office for Mr Choi. Mr Choi told the class to keep working while he was away, and he left them to it.

For a minute or two after he'd gone, the class carried on working. But then someone threw a paper-clip. Then someone else threw a jotter. And, a minute later, almost everyone was throwing things, standing on chairs, or fighting under the desks.

Arlo grinned. "This is better than doing rotten sums," he said.

"Anything's better than sums," Brin agreed. He waved his hands at the board like a magician and hissed, "Vanish, sums!"

And that was when the first strange thing happened. The sums dribbled down the board, ran off the bottom, and fell into a heap on the floor, where they faded to minus nothing.

Brin and Arlo just stared – first at the blank board, then at one another.

"Uh?" they said.

Then someone else saw the board. "What happened to the sums?" they asked.

And then someone else. "Where did they go?"

Then everyone looked, and they all wondered the same thing. They were still wondering when Mr Choi returned and asked crossly who had rubbed his sums off. When no one admitted to having done it, he gave the whole class extra Maths homework.

Chapter 2
Stranger Still

The next strange thing happened in Art. Mrs Mellor had set up a still-life for everyone to draw. It was of a bowl of fruit, a water jug, some dried flowers, and a folded scarf. Some of the girls thought it was quite an interesting still-life, but none of the boys did. Arlo waggled an annoyed hand and said that he wished Mrs Mellor would let them draw monsters instead.

"Today, class," Mrs Mellor said, "I want you all to draw monsters."

"Monsters?" someone said in amazement.

"And I want to see some really *horrible* ones, please," Mrs Mellor added. "Is that understood?"

They were all puzzled, but everyone was soon hard at work drawing the most horrible monsters they could imagine.

They drew blood-sucking vampires. They drew snarling werewolves. They drew demons with horns and claws. They drew staring zombies. They drew aliens with tentacles. They drew screaming skulls. They drew giant gorillas beating their chests. They drew ... well, you name it, as long as it was really horrible, the class drew it. It was the best time they'd ever had in Art.

After 20 minutes, Mrs Mellor began walking round looking at the drawings – and she was *horrified*.

"What are you all doing?" she cried.

"We're drawing monsters, Miss," the children said.

"Why are you drawing monsters? I told you to draw my still-life."

"No, you didn't. You said we had to draw monsters," they told her.

"Oh really! Why would I say something like that?" Mrs Mellor asked.

"Dunno, Miss, but you did."

At the end of the lesson, Brin and Arlo left the Art room in a daze.

"What happened back there?" said Brin.

"I don't even want to think about it," said Arlo.

It was during lunch break that the third strange thing happened. Most of the school ate lunch in the canteen. School meals were quite healthy these days, and most of the students liked them. But Brin and Arlo were among those who didn't really like curry, nut cutlets, salad and vegetarian pasta.

Brin waved his hand in despair at the serving counters.

"Why can't it be beans, chips and burgers, and treacle pudding and chocolate sauce, like we used to have?" he said.

He'd hardly finished speaking when a gasp went up from the children in front of them. Brin and Arlo craned their necks to see what had made everyone gasp, and they saw the food that had been put on some of the plates.

"Beans, chips, burgers, treacle pudding and chocolate sauce!" Brin cried.

"And all on the same plate!" Arlo said.

Some students were pretty confused about this and some didn't fancy such a mixture. But Brin and Arlo took two unwanted plates and carried them to a table well away from everyone else. While teachers and canteen staff scratched their heads about the shocking change that had come over the food, the twins ate up. Chips went quite well with treacle pudding, they found. And as for baked beans in chocolate sauce ...

"These things that are happening," said Arlo as they tucked in. "You don't think they're anything to do with us, do you?"

"Us?" said Brin.

"Well, think about it. What was the first weird thing that happened?"

"The sums vanished from Mr Choi's board," Brin said.

"Yes. After you wished they would."

"Just a fluke," Brin muttered as he stuffed another chip in his mouth.

"And what about Art? Mrs Mellor set up a still-life. Then she told us to draw monsters instead – right after I wished we could. And she didn't even remember *telling* us to draw them!"

"I don't get it," Brin said.

"Me neither," said Arlo. "But this food's great!"

The main lesson after lunch was Games. For this, the girls went off with Mrs Cork and the boys went with Mr Antony.

The school sports day was coming up, so they had to practise the events they would be taking part in, such as the long jump, the high jump and the relay race. The twins were as good or as bad as one another at everything. They were getting ready for the 400 metres race with a number of other boys.

"I hate running," Brin grumbled as everyone got ready at the starting blocks. "Wish we could speed it up and get it over with."

"Maybe we can," said Arlo.

"How?" Brin asked.

"Well, if we really can make weird things happen ..."

Because the twins thought so much alike, Brin knew exactly what Arlo meant. He smiled, and the two of them said in a whisper, "When Mr Antony blows the whistle we're going to run like *racehorses*!" And they waggled their fingers as if they were making magic.

"Ready, lads?" Mr Antony said.

All the boys at the starting blocks bent over and put their hands on the ground. Then Mr Antony blew his whistle. The boys galloped off like *racehorses*!

"Maybe we should have just said to run fast, not like horses," panted Brin as they galloped over the finish line.

"Never mind," said Arlo as they stood upright again. "That proves it. It's us that's making the weird stuff happen!"

"Yeah." Brin grinned from ear to ear. "Fantastic!"

Chapter 3
Truths About Magic

At home, after school, the twins told Ellie all that had happened during the day. She didn't believe a word at first. But then a friend (who was in Brin and Arlo's class) phoned her about the vanishing sums, the Art teacher telling her students to draw monsters, the change that came over the food in the canteen, and the boys galloping like horses around the playing field.

"All right, so some crazy stuff went down today," Ellie said after she'd hung up. "But that doesn't mean you two made it happen."

"I'm afraid it does," said a voice behind them. Their dad had just come in with the shopping.

"Do you know what this is all about?" Arlo asked him.

"Oh, I know all right," said Mr Pertinax.

"Tell us then," said Brin.

"I will. When your mother gets home."

When Mrs Pertinax came home from work, Mr Pertinax took her to one side and told her what he'd heard the children talking about.

"It's happened," Mrs Pertinax said, going pale. "Just as we feared it might."

Mr Pertinax nodded glumly.

When the tea was on the table and the family was sitting down, Mr Pertinax began his tale.

"As you know," he said, "we moved to the village of Witch Haven just after Ellie was born. We moved there in the hope of living a normal life, which hadn't always been easy. You see, I come from a long line of wizards."

"Wizards?" all three children said together.

"Wizards. In the olden days, Pertinax wizards were in great demand. We were hired by kings and great lords to protect them and bring about the defeat of their enemies. But that was then. There's not much demand for wizards in the 21st century, apart from in stories and at the cinema. It's a bit tricky sometimes."

"Tricky?" said Brin.

"Not to do magic. I try to keep it to myself, but when you're a born wizard, the magic has a way of coming out every now and then whether you mean it to or not."

"Pull the other one, Dad," said Ellie. "You, a wizard? Ha!"

Her mother frowned. "Ellie," she said. "Every word of what your father says is true."

"So how come we've never seen him do magic then?" Ellie asked.

"Because he's gone out of his way to keep it from you, that's why," her mum said.

"Keep it from us?" said Arlo. "Why? Magic is so cool!" Unlike Ellie, he had no problem believing their parents.

Nor did Brin. "Show us some magic, Dad," he said.

"I suppose I must, to prove it to you," said Mr Pertinax. He looked around until his eyes fell on a vase of flowers on a small table under the window. He frowned, winked, and waved a hand. The flowers, the vase and the table turned into a coat-stand.

"Wow!" said Brin and Arlo, and even Ellie's mouth fell open.

"Simple party trick," their father said. "But when you can do such things with ease, you have to be on your toes all the time in case you make something happen while you're thinking of something else."

"Which is what caused our problems at Witch Haven," his wife said. "A few bits of magic done by mistake – a brilliant rainbow springing up on a cloudy day, someone's nose growing when they tell lies – and people begin to wonder who's to blame."

"Is that why we had to move?" Brin asked.

"It is. Gossip started about us and we were getting odd looks in the street. Then, finally … you remember the night the brick came through the window?"

At the time, Mr and Mrs Pertinax had told the children that yobs had been throwing bricks at a few houses in the village.

"You don't mean it was just our window?" Ellie said.

"I do," her mother said. "What you didn't notice – we hid it so you wouldn't worry – was that there was a note around the brick."

"A note? What did it say?" Ellie asked.

"It said, 'Go home, aliens.'"

Brin frowned. "Aliens? We're not aliens."

"We are different, which means the same thing to some people. After that, we knew we had to start again somewhere else. So we moved here. But after today ..."

"After today, what?" Ellie asked.

"Well, it seems that I've passed on the wizard gene to the boys. We hoped I hadn't. It misses the odd Pertinax male, you see. But events at school today show that it was a forlorn hope."

"You mean we *did* do magic?" Arlo said.

"I'm afraid you did."

The twins stared at one another.

"I don't get it," said Ellie. "If this is true, why did it start today? I mean, why *today*?"

Mrs Pertinax explained. "If the wizard gene is going to come out, it starts the day a male of the line reaches eleven years and six months old exactly. That's why we were nervous this morning. It turns out that we were right to be."

"I wonder if the boys can be taught to control it?" Mr Pertinax said, looking at the twins. "Learn not to make magic when there's anyone about, I mean."

"But making magic would be fun!" cried Brin.

"It would also get us noticed," said Mrs Pertinax. "There would be photos in the papers, and we'd be on TV. People wouldn't leave us alone. They would try and drive us out, like last time."

"We have to give it a try," Mr Pertinax said. "When we've finished eating, you boys will go with me to the park, where I'll try to show you how to keep your magic to yourselves."

"It's not fair!" Ellie burst out. "Why should these two be able to do magic and not me? I'm the eldest."

"Ellie, listen to me," her mother said. "Magic is not a blessing. In today's world it's more trouble than it's worth. Even in the past, people who used it weren't always treated with respect. Take witches, for example."

"Witches?" Ellie asked.

"Many of them were drowned or burned at the stake."

Ellie stuck out her lower lip. "Wish I was a witch," she said.

"Don't say that!" Mrs Pertinax said sharply. "Wish to become a normal teenager and nothing more."

"Normal is boring," Ellie grumbled.

"At least people don't throw bricks at normal teenagers," her dad said.

"Most of the time," said Mrs Pertinax.

Chapter 4
Daisies and Dragons

Most of the park was open grassland. There were trees, of course, and bushes, and flowerbeds, and there was also a small lake, but that was about it. This made it the perfect place to practise magic. As luck would have it, there was no one else there that evening.

"I think the best thing," Mr Pertinax said to the twins, "is for me to show you the right way to make magic. Then you'll have some idea of what not to do when there are people about. Now, where shall we start ...?"

He looked about him and saw that the grass around a nearby oak tree was thick with little white daisies.

"You see those daisies?" Mr Pertinax said. "What I'd like you to do is make them grow. I mean, really grow."

"What for?" Brin asked.

"To see if you can."

"Can't we do something else?" Arlo asked. "Something interesting, like, say, make thunder. Or lightning."

"All in good time," said Mr Pertinax. "For now, let's see if you can make daisies grow."

"How do we do it?" asked Arlo.

"Well, to start with, you point at them."
Mr Pertinax held up the index finger of his
right hand. "This is a wizard's pointing
finger," he said. "The rest of the fingers are
used to make other kinds of magic, but for the
moment let's see what you can do with this
one."

Brin and Arlo pointed at the daisies around
the oak tree.

"Now close your eyes and focus on making
them grow really tall," Mr Pertinax said.

"We didn't focus when we made that stuff
happen at school," said Brin.

"Maybe not, but you weren't in control
then either. Control is very important. If
your hands and minds aren't focused on the
same thing, there can be odd side-effects."

The boys closed their eyes, tried to focus, and in half a minute some of the daises started to grow.

"Oh, well done, Arlo!" Mr Pertinax said.

Both boys opened their eyes.

"How do you know it was him and not me who did that?" Brin asked.

"I know because you weren't holding your finger still and you kept peeking."

"I'll try again then," Brin said.

Brin closed his eyes once more, but he was so excited by what he might do with these new powers that he couldn't keep the fingers of his other hand still. And ...

"Oh no!" cried Mr Pertinax.

Brin's eyelids snapped open. "What's up?"

"Look at the sky!" his dad said.

It had become dark and grim. And, as they looked, a bolt of white lightning zig-zagged out of it and struck the oak tree. There was a mighty crack, and a branch snapped and crashed to the ground.

"Well, you made your lightning after all," Mr Pertinax said. He didn't sound very pleased.

"You mean I did that?" said Brin in amazement.

"Yes. You did," his dad said. "And do you know why? Because you didn't keep your fingers under control while you focused. That was very foolish of you, Brin. If there'd been anyone about, they could have been badly hurt."

Brin looked down at his feet. "Sorry, Dad."

Mr Pertinax would have said more, but he was cut short by a sharp yapping sound and a spaniel that ran between them and cocked its leg against the daisies, which were now a metre high.

Arlo waved the small dog away. "Buzz off, you stupid mutt!"

The words were hardly out of his mouth when the dog lifted off the ground (spraying the giant daises as it did so), and its yap became a loud buzz. Then, flying through the air, it made a "bee line" for the lake.

"What's that mad mutt of mine up to now?" said the dog's owner, running up as the dog tumbled nose-first into the water.

"Looks like he wanted a paddle," Mr Pertinax said.

"From where I was standing it looked like he *flew* there!" the dog's owner said.

"Most likely it's just high spirits."

"Weird! Like those giant snap-dragons. And what about that lightning? Global warming has a lot to answer for, if you ask me!" the dog's owner said.

"What was that about snap-dragons?" Brin said, as they watched the man go after his dog.

This was answered by an angry snap-snap-snap sound behind them, followed by growls and hisses. Before the boys could turn to see what was there, the grass around their feet burst into flames.

"Run, boys, run!" cried their dad, grabbing each of them by an arm.

The twins looked over their shoulders as he rushed them away. The giant daises were giant daisies no longer. They were dragon heads on stalks – breathing fire!

"What happened to the daisies?" Arlo said.

"The dog weed on them," his father replied.

"So?"

"It was a spaniel."

"So?"

"Spaniel-widdle added to giant daisies changes the daisies into snap-dragons. If the dog had been a different breed, the result would have been different," Mr Pertinax said.

"Different how?" asked Brin.

"Well, if a wolf-hound had piddled on the daises they would have turned into enormous Venus Fly Traps, which could take your arm off. And if it had been a corgi we would now be looking at Scorpion Orchids – even more dangerous!"

"The flames are going out," Brin said, looking back.

And so they were. And the fire-breathing snap-dragons were turning back into daisies. And the daisies were shrinking back to normal size.

"I think we need to practise somewhere else," Mr Pertinax said. "Somewhere more private."

"Like where?" said Arlo.

"Like home."

"How did they get on?" Mrs Pertinax asked when they got home.

"Well, we've made a start," her husband said. "But for safety's sake, the next lesson is going to be given in our own back garden."

When he and the twins had gone out to the garden, Mrs Pertinax saw her daughter's down-turned mouth.

"Now what?" she asked.

"Same thing as before," Ellie said. "They've got magic and I haven't. I want to be a wizard too."

"Girls can't be wizards," her mother said.

"Well, I never asked to be a girl," Ellie replied.

"No, you didn't, but for your sake I hope that's all you ever are."

"What do you mean?" Ellie asked.

"I mean, don't you have homework that has to be in by Monday?" her mother said.

"I'll do it on Sunday," Ellie said. "If I were a *wizard* I'd make it do itself."

"You would not," Mrs Pertinax said. "House rule – no homework to be done by magic."

She repeated this for the boys when they came in a little later.

"Oh, Mum," said Brin. "What's the point of being able to do magic if you can't use it on your homework?"

"Don't argue," she said. "You'll do your homework the same way as everyone else. I will *not* have you using magic to cheat. Are they getting the hang of it?" she asked her husband.

"Well, they're not doing badly for beginners," he replied. "Even if Arlo did turn next door's greenhouse into an enormous pink rabbit. Good thing I was there to turn it back before someone saw it."

Ellie stuck her lower lip out. "Still not fair," she muttered.

"Be positive," her mum told her. "Think about tomorrow. The big day."

Ellie thought about tomorrow. It helped her get over her envy of her brothers. They might be young wizards, but she was the one who would be getting presents in the morning!

Chapter 5
More Truths About Magic

The next morning, Ellie came down in as cheerful a mood as any other birthday girl. The first thing her mother did when she saw her was ask if she felt any different.

"Well, I *feel* the same as yesterday," Ellie said. "But, Mum! I'm a teenager!"

"So you are, dear," her mother said, patting her hand.

As it wasn't a school morning there was no rush, so Ellie took her time opening her cards and gifts. The presents included a 1,000-piece jigsaw (Ellie loved jigsaws), a watch, a chunky necklace, and an iPod.

"Nothing from you two, as ever," Ellie said to the twins.

"The ones from your dad and me are also from Brin and Arlo," Mrs Pertinax reminded her.

"Yes, but that's only because they haven't bothered to get me anything," Ellie said.

The boys looked at one another. Did they have the heart to give her the "present" they'd wrapped up yesterday morning? One of them grinned. The other one grinned back. Of course they did!

"Don't go away," they said, and they scampered upstairs.

When they returned with their "gift", Ellie began to unwrap it. Brin and Arlo could hardly contain themselves as she did so.

"Pathetic!" Ellie said, when she saw what they'd given her.

"Oh, not that," Mrs Pertinax said. "Today of *all* days you shouldn't have given her *that*."

And suddenly, because no one saw the funny side, it didn't seem such a great joke to Brin and Arlo either. In fact, they felt rather stupid. They might have actually said sorry if something hadn't happened that made their jaws drop. And not just *their* jaws. Ellie, too, stared as the brush that belonged to the battered old dustpan changed shape and size and became an old-fashioned broom with a long wooden handle and a bundle of twigs at one end.

Ellie turned on the boys, waving the broom angrily at them.

"You two think you're so clever, don't you? Well, let me tell you, this is the first and last time you're using any of that wizardy stuff on me!"

She turned to the window, intending to throw the broom into the garden. But she didn't throw it. The broom threw itself, and because Ellie hadn't let go, it took her with it. And once outside, the broom flew up and up and up (taking her along for the ride), above the gardens and greenhouses and sheds and the roofs of all the houses.

Brin and Arlo rushed to the window. "How did we do that?" they gasped.

"You didn't," their father said, joining them. "Ellie did it herself."

"How could she do it herself? She's not a young wizard."

"Not a young wizard, no. She's a young witch," Mr Pertinax said.

The twins gasped. "A young *witch?*"

"Just as we hoped the wizard gene would have missed you two, we hoped your gran's witch gene would miss Ellie," Mr Pertinax said.

"Witch gene?" said Arlo. "You mean Gran was a witch?"

"Yes."

"She didn't look like one," Brin said.

"Not all witches have hooked noses and warts and cackle a lot," Mr Pertinax said. "She had her days, though, being my mother-in-law."

"But if Gran was a witch and Ellie's a witch, doesn't that mean that you're one too?" Brin said to his mother.

Mrs Pertinax shook her head. "A daughter of a witch can never become one. But a grand-daughter can. It doesn't always happen, but it *can*."

"And it clearly has in Ellie's case," said Mr Pertinax.

"But she wasn't a witch yesterday," said Arlo.

"She wasn't 13 yesterday. When a witch's grand-daughter turns 13, she either becomes a normal teenager or a witch like her. We would have settled for the normal teenager."

"That broom ..." Brin said, watching his sister flying around the roof-tops holding onto the handle for dear life.

"It was my mum's," said Mrs Pertinax. "When she died, it changed itself into a normal sweeping brush because there was no one to use it. Ellie's 13th birthday witch-touch must have woken it up. Made it want to stretch its twigs."

"I hope she can keep hold of it," said Mr Pertinax, staring up into the sky.

"It won't let her fall," his wife said. "It's hers now. It'll look after her."

"She's coming back!" Brin and Arlo cried.

And indeed she was. The broomstick (which Ellie was now riding rather than simply hanging onto) had swung around in the sky and was heading for the house.

They all stepped away from the window just in time. Ellie landed on the carpet with a bump. Her hair was all over the place and she was goggle-eyed, but thrilled.

"What a ride!" she said, getting off the broomstick. She turned to the twins. "Maybe I will let you do that again every now and then."

"It wasn't the boys," her mother said.

"What do you mean, it wasn't the boys? Who else could have made it happen? Unless ..." Ellie looked at her father.

He held his hands up. "It wasn't me."

"Ellie," Mrs Pertinax said. "We have something to tell you."

And Ellie heard how, overnight, she had become a witch. At first she was horrified.

"Me? A witch? What will my friends say?"

"Your friends mustn't know," her mother said. "It must remain a family secret. I'm sorry about this, dear. I wish the witch gene had missed you, but it hasn't, so the best thing you can do is to stay away from that broomstick and not even *think* about casting spells."

Ellie's eyes widened. "I can cast *spells?*"

"Yes, of course, but as I say, you must do nothing of the kind – not if you want to be a normal teenager."

But Ellie had stopped listening. She was muttering a spell she'd recently heard in a film about witches. At the same time, she waved her hands at a framed photo of her gran.

"Hi, Ellie!" said Gran.

The picture had come to life. Gran leaned out of the frame, smiling – but just for a few seconds, before she sank back and became a photo again.

Ellie grinned. "I cast a spell! And it worked!"

"We can do better than that," said Arlo.

He pointed at the TV and closed his eyes. Almost at once the TV became a full-grown tiger, eager for fresh meat. It roared and started towards them. It was a good thing that Mr Pertinax had his wits about him. He raised a hand, waggled an eyebrow, and the hungry tiger became a tiger on the screen again, running after a herd of deer.

"Oh, that's nothing," Ellie said. "Watch this!"

She uttered another spell, a made-up one this time, and the 1,000 pieces of her new jigsaw jumped out of the box and, hanging in mid-air, slotted themselves together.

"No magic in the house!" Mrs Pertinax shouted.

"Come on," said Brin. "Outside!"

As the jigsaw fell into a thousand pieces on the carpet, the young wizards and the young

witch ran into the garden to see what spells they could cast, what magic they could make.

Their parents sank onto the sofa.

"Oh dear," said Mr Pertinax.

"Oh dear indeed," said Mrs Pertinax. "So much for being like everyone else. We'd better put the house up for sale. Time to move on – again!"

Our books are tested
for children and young people by
children and young people.

Thanks to everyone who consulted on
a manuscript for their time and effort in
helping us to make our books better
for our readers.